A Visit to CHILE

by Charis Mather

Minneapolis, Minnesota

Credits

All images are courtesy of Shutterstock.com, unless otherwise specified. With thanks to Getty Images, Thinkstock Photo, and iStockphoto.

Cover - JeremyRichards, Dudarev Mikhail. 2-3 - Jose Luis Stephens. 4-5 - Always Wanderlust. 6-7 - Gil C, Pablo Rogat. 8-9 - erlucho, carriagada, Marco Aurelio JR. 10-11 - Papa Bravo, DaryaU. 12-13 - Delpixel, Natursports. 14-15 - Dave Primov, Brian Maudsley. 16-17 - Melinda Nagy, Carlos Figueroa Rojas, abriendomundo. 18-19 - Vlad Vahnovan, DMITRII SIMAKOV. 20-21 - Ildi Papp, hlphoto. 22-23 - David Ionut, f11photo.

Library of Congress Cataloging-in-Publication Data is available at www.loc.gov or upon request from the publisher.

ISBN: 979-8-88509-037-7 (hardcover)
ISBN: 979-8-88509-048-3 (paperback)
ISBN: 979-8-88509-059-9 (ebook)

© 2023 Booklife Publishing
This edition is published by arrangement with Booklife Publishing.

North American adaptations © 2023 Bearport Publishing Company. All rights reserved. No part of this publication may be reproduced in whole or in part, stored in any retrieval system, or transmitted in any form or by any means, electronic, mechanical, photocopying, recording, or otherwise, without written permission from the publisher.

For more information, write to Bearport Publishing, 5357 Penn Avenue South, Minneapolis, MN 55419. Printed in the United States of America.

CONTENTS

Country to Country 4

Today's Trip Is to Chile! 6

Santiago 8

The Andes 10

Atacama Desert 12

Animals 14

Activities 16

Festivals 18

Food 20

Before You Go 22

Glossary 24

Index 24

COUNTRY TO COUNTRY

A country is an area of land marked by **borders**. The people in each country have their own rules and ways of living. They may speak different languages.

Which country do you live in?

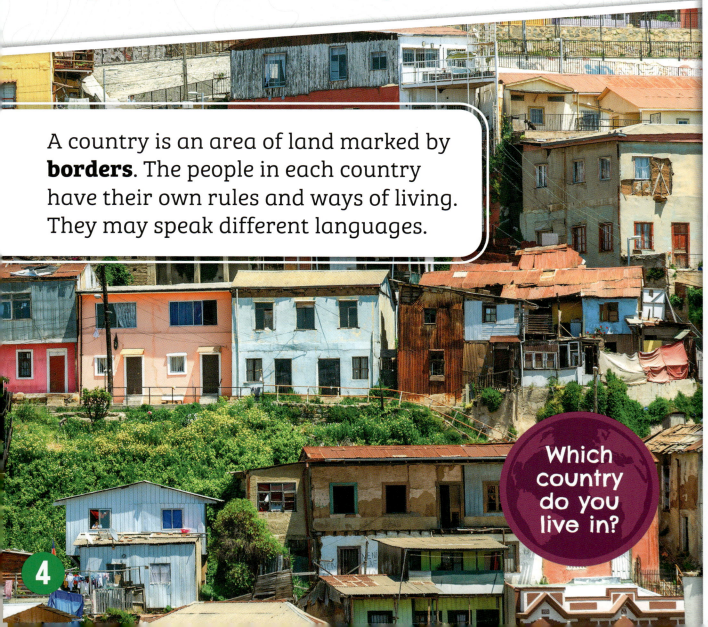

Each country around the world has its own interesting things to see and do. Let's take a trip to visit a country and learn more!

Have you ever visited another country?

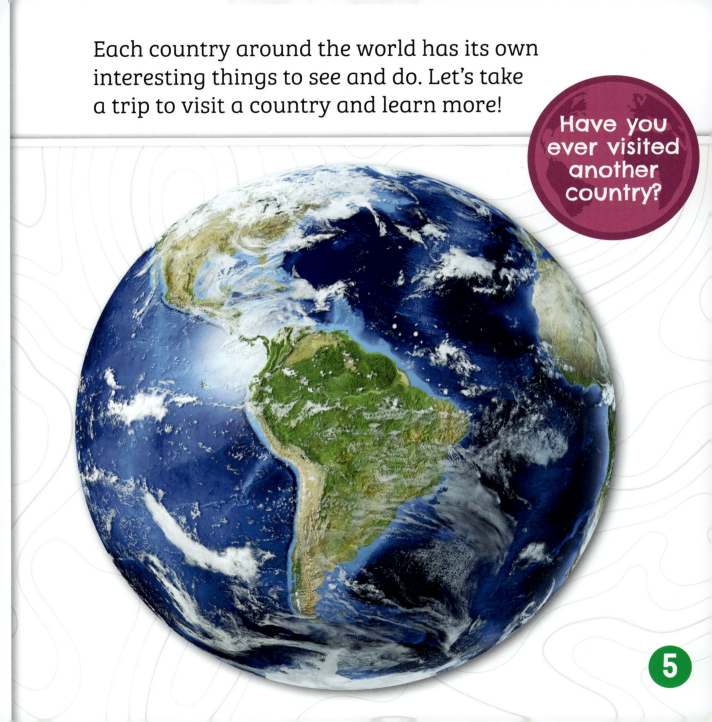

TODAY'S TRIP IS TO
CHILE!

Chile is a country in the **continent** of South America.

FACT FILE

Capital city: Santiago
Main language: Spanish
Currency: Chilean peso
Flag:

Currency is the type of money that is used in a country.

SANTIAGO

We'll start our trip in Santiago, the capital city of Chile. From the top of the Sky Costanera, we can see the city in every direction. The Sky Costanera is one of the tallest buildings in South America.

Sky Costanera

San Cristóbal Hill

San Cristóbal Hill is another great place for cool views of the city. It is in one of Santiago's many parks. We can ride to the top of the hill in a **railcar**.

THE ANDES

There is snow on the Andes Mountains.

Santiago is not the only place in Chile with great views. The country also has beautiful mountains called the Andes. They stretch over 5,530 miles (8,900 km).

10

Many of the mountains in the Andes are **volcanoes.** In fact, one of the tallest volcanoes in the world is in Chile! It is called Ojos del Salado, and it is more than 22,300 feet (6,800 m) tall.

Ojos del Salado

ATACAMA DESERT

The Andes Mountains keep rain clouds from moving over the Atacama Desert. This is one of the driest places in the world.

The Atacama Desert has many flat areas covered in salt.

Because it is so dry, a lot of plants and animals cannot live there. But unlike many deserts, the Atacama Desert is not extremely hot. Its average temperature is about 63 degrees Fahrenheit (18 degrees Celsius).

ANIMALS

Guanacos

Next, let's meet some animals! Chile is home to guanacos. These animals are similar to camels and llamas. They can run faster than 30 miles per hour (50 kph).

Along the **coast** of Chile, we can find Humboldt penguins. They are good at climbing on the slippery rocks along the water. Humboldt penguins can be recognized by the pink patches near their eyes.

Humboldt penguins

ACTIVITIES

Ready for some fun? Let's go play soccer! This is one of Chile's most popular sports. But in Chile, soccer is called football.

The Cueca

Chile also has a **national** dance called the Cueca. Cueca dancers hold up pieces of cloth to make themselves look like birds waving their feathers. Sometimes, they wear **traditional** clothes.

FESTIVALS

Fiestas Patrias is on September 18.

Chile's most important **festival** is Fiestas Patrias. It is Chile's **Independence** Day. People eat lots of food and enjoy watching sports and Cueca dances.

During the We Tripantu festival, the local Mapuche people celebrate the new year with a big bonfire. At the Grape Harvest Festival, people celebrate that grapes are ready to be picked. They stomp on the fruit to make juice.

We Tripantu

Grape Harvest Festival

FOOD

Feeling hungry? Let's grab some food. First, we'll try sopaipillas (SO-pye-PEE-yuhs), a type of fried snack. Chilean people make sopaipillas with pumpkin and sometimes eat them with a sweet sauce or a tomato dish.

Sopaipilla

Empanadas are another popular food in Chile. This fried bread is stuffed with different fillings. The fillings may include beef, cheese, olives, raisins, or boiled eggs.

BEFORE YOU GO

Torres del Paine National Park

We can't forget to see Torres del Paine National Park! This place has beautiful mountains, lakes, and rivers. Many people visit to see the park's three mountaintops.

We could also head to Valparaíso. This bright city is right next to the ocean and has lots of colorful old buildings.

What have you learned about Chile on this trip?

GLOSSARY

borders lines that show where one place ends and another begins

coast an area where land meets an ocean

continent one of the world's seven large land masses

festival an event where many people come together to celebrate

independence when a place is no longer controlled by another country

national having to do with a country

railcar a cart that runs on railroad tracks and can carry passengers

traditional relating to something that a group of people has done for many years

volcanoes mountains that can erupt to let out hot, melted rock

INDEX

buildings 8, 23
continents 6
dances 17–18

Fiestas Patrias 18
grapes 19
Mapuche people 19

mountains 10–12, 22
sports 16, 18
We Tripantu 19